The Banana-Leaf Ball

To my life coaches: Michael, Brendan, Mary Kate and Sophie — K.S.M.

I thank God for the gift of creativity. I dedicate this book to the Love Light within us all and special thanks to Mama C, Brother Pete and UAACC for all they do. — S.W.E.

ACKNOWLEDGMENTS

My inspiration for this book came from multiple sources: my colleague Taz Hussein at The Bridgespan Group, an advocate of the "power of play" to improve the health of youth and communities; my long-time Kids Can Press editor Val Wyatt, who suggested I look at the work of global NGO Right To Play; and Johann Koss, Right To Play's founder, who introduced me to a speech given by Benjamin Nzobonankira, which informs the narrative of this book. Benjamin himself became a long-distance friend from Burundi, correcting Kirundi expressions and filling in details of Lukole life. And his story connected to my own experiences working for NGO Food for the Hungry in refugee camps, volunteering with nonprofit program One Hen in urban after-school programs, and coaching for Wellesley United Soccer Club as a parent of three players. I am grateful for the many organizations focused on putting sport in the service of social and emotional learning, and that the power of play has grown my own children's resilience, self-esteem and regard for others. I'm also grateful that the power of playing with words enabled my current editor, Stacey Roderick, to work magic on the manuscript!

Kids Can Press gratefully acknowledges the financial support of the Government of Ontario, through the Ontario Media Development Corporation; the Ontario Arts Council; the Canada Council for the Arts; and the Government of Canada, through the CBF, for our publishing activity.

Published in Canada and the U.S. by Kids Can Press Ltd.
25 Dockside Drive, Toronto, ON M5A 0B5

Kids Can Press is a Corus Entertainment Inc. company

www.kidscanpress.com

Edited by Valerie Wyatt and Stacey Roderick
Designed by Marie Bartholomew

Printed and bound in Shenzhen, China, in 3/2018 through Asia Pacific Offset

CM 17 0 9 8 7 6 5 4 3

FSC
www.fsc.org
MIX
Paper from responsible sources
FSC® C012521

Library and Archives Canada Cataloguing in Publication

Milway, Katie Smith, 1960–, author
　The banana-leaf ball : how play can change the world / written by Katie Smith Milway ; illustrated by Shane W. Evans.

(CitizenKid)
ISBN 978-1-77138-331-8 (hardback)

　1. Soccer — Juvenile fiction. 2. Refugee camps — Tanzania — Juvenile fiction. 3. Bullying — Juvenile fiction. 4. Children and war — Juvenile fiction. I. Evans, Shane W., illustrator II. Title. III. Series: CitizenKid

PS8626.I48B36 2017　jC813'.6　C2016-903375-9

THE BANANA-LEAF BALL

How Play Can Change the World

KATIE SMITH MILWAY

SHANE W. EVANS

CitizenKid™

A collection of books that inform children about the
world and inspire them to be better global citizens

Kids Can Press

Deo Rukundo didn't know why the war began in his country. But he knew that one dark night his family was forced to flee their hillside farm and its terraces of sweet potatoes, beans and bananas.

Deo wanted to bring his favorite toy, a soccer ball he'd woven from banana leaves. He was the best player of all his friends. But his father told him, "*Ejo.*" Tomorrow he could make a new one. Tonight, only pots, blankets and food would fit on their small cart.

As his family hurried down a path, more farmers joined them. Suddenly, men with torches and machetes exploded out of the dark. They set fire to huts and carts and attacked the farmers. Deo's father shouted, "*Genda! Genda!*" Go! Go!

When Deo finally stopped running, deep in the forest, he was alone and very frightened.

6

Now Deo lives in Lukole, a refugee camp in northwest Tanzania.

For weeks he had traveled alone through the dark forest. Staying hidden by day and running at night, he survived only on dewdrops, wild fruits and leaves. At last, Deo came to a great lake, and a fisherman found him, just skin and bones, and brought him across to this place.

The camp is dusty, and each day he uses a tap to fill one can of water for bathing, cleaning and drinking. He also receives one meal a day. There are huts made of plastic sheeting that he and thousands of other refugees call home. He misses his family and prays they are safe.

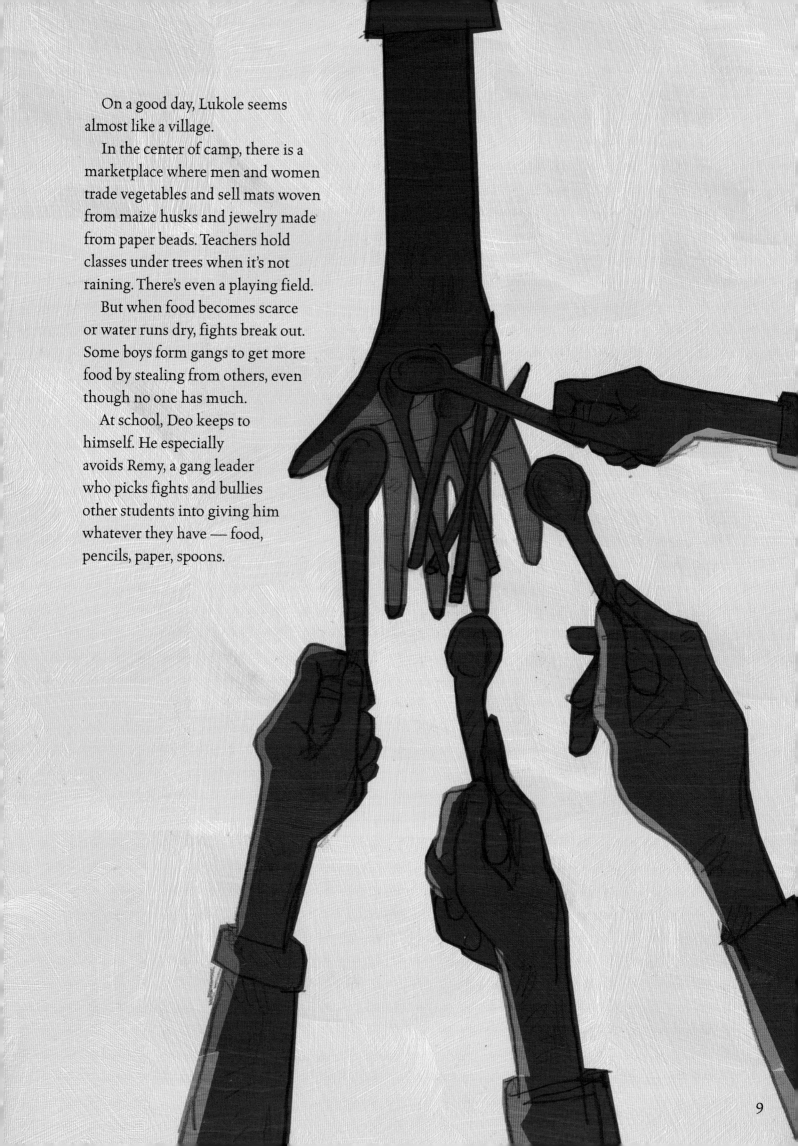

On a good day, Lukole seems almost like a village.

In the center of camp, there is a marketplace where men and women trade vegetables and sell mats woven from maize husks and jewelry made from paper beads. Teachers hold classes under trees when it's not raining. There's even a playing field.

But when food becomes scarce or water runs dry, fights break out. Some boys form gangs to get more food by stealing from others, even though no one has much.

At school, Deo keeps to himself. He especially avoids Remy, a gang leader who picks fights and bullies other students into giving him whatever they have — food, pencils, paper, spoons.

Deo longs for the time he used to spend playing soccer with friends. One day, he remembers his father's words from the night they fled and begins to make twine from dried banana leaves to bind up a new ball.

While he sits outside his hut twisting leaves, Remy and his gang storm over. One boy pins Deo's arms behind his back. Deo struggles, but Remy grabs the twine and runs off, laughing.

Deo goes inside his hut, blinking back tears. He kicks at his pile of banana leaves drying on the mud floor.

The next day, Deo stays indoors. First he twists more leaves into twine. Then he wraps layer upon layer of leaves into a big, round bundle. He ties the twine around it, crisscrossing the cords to hold the ball's shape. Passing it back and forth between his hands, Deo can tell it's a good ball. He decides to hide it.

A little later, Deo hears a commotion. When he looks out, a man with a whistle around his neck is striding down the path. Children from the camp are following, shouting and laughing. The man holds a ball — not one made from banana leaves, but from leather.

Deo joins the crowd. Arriving at the playing field, he sees Remy and his friends. Remy makes a face at Deo and lifts his T-shirt; the twine he stole is holding up his shorts.

Suddenly, the stranger blows his whistle, throws the soccer ball in the air and bounces it from his forehead to his knees and then to his feet.

"*Mwaramutse?*" the coach says in
Kirundi to a group of youngsters. "Do
you want to play?"

"*Ego! Ego!*" Yes! Yes!

Deo wants to join, too, but he isn't sure.
He sees boys and girls across the field,
watching and talking excitedly. He also
sees Remy, his arms crossed, quiet for
once. Just as Deo turns to walk away, the
coach shouts and throws him the ball.

Without thinking, Deo catches it
on one knee and bounces it knee to
knee, foot to foot and down to the
ground. "Great!" says the coach.
"You can be captain of the Shirts
team, so keep yours on."

"And you can be captain of the
Skins," the coach tells a quiet, sturdy
boy named Yvan, who quickly sheds
his shirt.

Then the coach begins to sort the
rest of the boys into teams. When he
gets to Remy, he says, "You join the
Shirts."

Remy comes up behind Deo and squeezes the back of his neck hard. "We better win," he snarls.

But first the coach wants the teams to warm up. They form two lines facing each other on either end of a row of sticks. Deo starts off, dribbling the ball between the sticks to the other end of the field. Then he passes the ball to Yvan, who brings it back and kicks it to the next player. Deo watches when it's Remy's turn. He is pretty fast.

Finally, it's time to play! The coach has each team take a side of the field. The whistle blows, and the center for the Shirts kicks the ball to Deo.

Deo dribbles it fast, right past Yvan. When another Skin runs at him, Deo fakes a kick and knocks the ball sideways around him. An elbow jabs his side, and Deo catches a glimpse of one of Remy's gang. Then someone trips him, and he sprawls in the dust. The whistle blows.

"Foul!" shouts the coach. "Shirts get a free kick."

Deo picks himself up quickly and sees Remy standing open. Without thinking, Deo kicks him the ball. Remy catches it on his knee and starts dribbling toward the goal.

Remy is closing in on the goal, but so are two Skins. From the corner of his eye, he sees Deo and shoots the ball sideways. Deo catches it with his foot and kicks it high toward the goal. Remy jumps up and knocks it with his head, right past the goalie. The Shirts score!

When the game is over, Deo's team has won by a point! Everyone is out of breath, tired and happy. Remy squeezes Deo's neck again, but more gently this time. "We did it," he says.

Soon all the Shirts have their arms around one another, singing a victory song, stomping the ground and laughing. The Skins gather, too, and joke that it was a lucky goal, that they will win next time.

"Great game!" says the coach. "*Ejo*, tomorrow, we'll switch around the teams!"

Walking back to their huts, Remy says he used to play soccer with his brothers, before he lost them in the war. This makes Deo think of his own family.

"*Urabizi!* You're good," Remy tells Deo. "Can you show me your tricks?"

Deo thinks for a moment and then replies, softly, "*Ego*. Yes. I have a ball we can use."

The next morning, Deo brings his banana-leaf ball out from its hiding place. He shows the other boys some of his best moves. Then Remy shows everyone how to loft the ball high over someone's head. He kicks it so hard a piece of twine breaks.

"Don't worry," Remy shouts, running after the ball. "We have more twine!" Taking the cord from his shorts, he gives it back to Deo.

Smiling, Deo makes a quick repair. The scrimmage is on!

Remy comes by Deo's hut later. "That was fun," he says. "Can you show me how to make one of those balls?"

For the rest of the morning they twist twine and bundle leaves, all the while talking about the homes and families they miss. Before long, others come by Deo's hut for lessons and conversation.

Months pass, and the boys of Lukole keep making banana-leaf balls and playing together. Ball by ball, practice by practice, children who were once afraid of one another laugh together. There are still problems in the camp, but no one feels so alone anymore. They are like a team, and their hope for *ejo*, tomorrow, is becoming hope for *ubu*, now.

A few years later, it is safe for Deo, Remy and the other refugees from the camp to return home, and Lukole closes. Deo is overjoyed to find members of his family who had been living in another camp. They rebuild a home together on the plot of land they once farmed and replant crops of sweet potatoes, beans and bananas.

But Deo can't farm every day because now *he* is a coach. Each Friday he goes to a local school to help children learn to play together and trust one another. He also teaches them how to make banana-leaf balls.

Today he arrives to find two boys fighting. He thinks back to his first game at Lukole and blows his whistle. Then he tosses a ball to one of them. "*Hoji!* Let's play!"

A Real Deo

Today almost 60 million people are refugees — men, women and children who have had to leave their homes because of war or disaster. Many live in, or have lived in, temporary camps around the world.

Much of this story is based on the experiences of one such boy, Benjamin Nzobonankira from Burundi, a country in East Africa. In 1993, ten-year-old Benjamin and his family had to flee their home when conflict broke out. For months he traveled through the forest, at times surviving on rainwater, wild fruits and leaves. Like Deo, Benjamin eventually became separated from his entire family.

After a long and very difficult journey, Benjamin finally found himself in Lukole, the setting for *The Banana-Leaf Ball*, in a refugee camp run by the United Nations, an organization made up of many countries working to improve human rights and reduce conflict. In Lukole, Benjamin was overjoyed to be reunited with his father and some cousins, though grief-stricken that his mother and sister did not survive their escape.

Although comfortable compared to other camps, Lukole had its troubles with gangs and a lack of resources, and Benjamin still wished for stability and safety. But life there got better for Benjamin in 2001 when a coach from Right To Play arrived. Right To Play is an organization that uses sport and play to educate and empower children and youth to overcome the effects of poverty, disease and conflict. They believe play

can teach children how to protect themselves from disease, encourage them to attend and stay in school, and model ways to resolve conflict to create a peaceful community.

Benjamin used his childhood passion of weaving banana leaves into soccer balls and joined a Right To Play team. He found that playing sports was the only thing that gave him relief and let him relax. While playing, he and his friends were able to laugh and have fun. Eventually Benjamin became a Right To Play volunteer in the camp, and as he coached others, he found his confidence and his tolerance for differences growing. He began to look to the future, to build his skills and to set goals.

In 2008, Lukole camp closed and Benjamin finally returned home. There he began to organize activities for children in his community to help them learn tolerance and confidence through the power of play, too. He even rose to lead Right To Play's national training team in Burundi, training 520 coaches who support 35 000 youth, changing fear and distrust on playgrounds into empathy and teamwork.

Expressions in Kirundi, the language of Burundi

Ego: Yes
Ejo: Tomorrow
Genda!: Go!
Hoji!: Let's play!
Mwaramutse?: Do you want to play?
Ubu: Now
Urabizi!: You're good

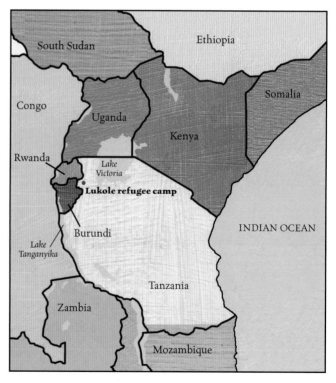

East Africa

Former child refugee Benjamin Nzobonankira coaching children.

A collection of banana-leaf balls.

How Kids Are Learning to Trust and Include Others

The problem of kids fearing each other also happens in places other than refugee camps. In fact, in schools around the world even recess can feel dangerous or unwelcoming, particularly to kids who are being bullied or left out. But with some coaching, playgrounds can be wonderful places to play. And through playing, kids learn how to make friends, lead others and build trust. Good sport can lead to good thinking, good health and good friendships. The following six organizations around the world use soccer and other forms of play to build compassion and confidence in boys and girls. You can try out their games on your own playground. And you can support these organizations by going to their websites and getting ideas for fundraisers.

Right To Play

www.righttoplay.com

Right To Play's 14 400 volunteer coaches reach more than one million children around the world through weekly sport and play programs. Right To Play games help kids do better in school, teach them health lessons and provide them with the skills to be peacemakers.

This Right To Play game is a fun way to build concentration and memory.

Remember Me
- Students are paired off with a few minutes to study one another.
- Then they stand facing away from one another, and each player alters his appearance: some players might change their hairstyle, while others roll up a sleeve or take off a shoe.
- When the coach says, "Go," the pairs turn to face one another and try to identify what has changed. Each player gets five guesses.
- The coach asks players how they remembered the way their partner looked at the start, and to think about a different time when they forgot something important and how they felt. Each player identifies ways to remember things better.

Taking time out to "Reflect, Connect, Apply" follows all Right To Play activities. This allows the children to *Reflect* on the lessons they just learned, *Connect* lessons to their daily life and *Apply* lessons to future situations.

Playworks

www.playworks.org

PW works with schools in twenty-one states across the United States to provide recess coaches who help kids learn fairness, become leaders and settle their disputes quickly — skills they will also carry into their classes and their neighborhoods.

Here's a game from their free Game Guide (www.playworks.org/playbook/games/get-the-game-guide) that helps kids learn to solve disagreements peacefully.

Switch
- Review the rules for rock-paper-scissors (see www.playworks.org/playbook/games/ro-sham-bo-or-rock-paper-scissors). Then make a square on the ground using markers such as cones, Hula-Hoops or chalk to mark four zones. Place a fifth marker in the middle.
- Have one player stand in each zone. Play begins when the person in the middle says, "Switch."
- All players must move to a new zone; no player can go to the center.
- If two players arrive at the same zone, they play a quick rock-paper-scissors game. The

winner stays and the other player goes to the back of the line.

- The next person in line goes to the middle marker to call "Switch" and begin the next round.

America SCORES

www.americascores.org

America SCORES is an after-school program that provides soccer, poetry and service-learning activities for ten thousand poet-athletes in the United States and Canada. SCORES uses this game to foster working together — no equipment required.

Traffic Jam

- Two teams of six to ten players form a circle by holding hands and spreading out, with each team on opposite sides of the circle. At a coach's command, everyone starts jogging in a circle.
- When the coach calls, "Traffic jam," all players run across the circle to the opposite side and relink hands. The coach times how fast they can all work together to build the new circle.
- Repeat, adding new commands for travel, such as "Jumping jacks," "Hop on one foot," "Hands up high," etc.

Gonzo Soccer

www.gonzosoccer.org

Gonzo Soccer is a nonprofit that runs soccer academies in the United States, Mexico and Colombia. It has become a place urban adolescent girls are given academic support and also learn life skills that will help them stay in school, find a place to belong and feel a sense of empowerment.

Here's a game that focuses on building bonds between teammates, setting the stage for compassion and cooperation.

Mind Buddies

- Beginning 15 m (16 yd.) out from a goal, place four cones in a line leading to the goal.
- Each player chooses a partner and the pair lie on their backs, side by side. Players close their eyes, relax and focus on their breathing for one minute. Players then sit back-to-back

and focus on their partner's breathing (with the goal of having their breathing become synchronized).

- Finally, partners face one another, eyes open. No communication is allowed. Players should notice their breathing, as well as any feelings or emotions that come up (feel free to "reflect" on these afterward as a team).
- One partner will now close her eyes (or be blindfolded) and attempt to dribble a soccer ball through a set of cones and score a goal with the help of her partner's instruction. Players then take turns.
- As a variation, you can place cones in a zigzag or create your own challenging obstacle course!

Grassroot Soccer (GRS)

www.grassrootsoccer.org

GRS uses the power of play to educate students about healthy behaviors. It partners with the Peace Corps and other organizations in seventeen developing countries, with a focus on Africa. It also works with student groups around the world to create twenty-four-hour barefoot soccer tournaments (learn more by visiting www.3v3pickup.org).

This GRS game builds awareness of how unfair behavior can affect others.

Fair Field

- Players (a minimum of nine and a maximum of eighteen) form three lines. Each line of players has a row of traffic cones in front of it, and each cone has a label stating an unfair behavior — for example, not telling the truth, taking advantage of others or breaking rules.

- Round 1: One at a time, each team member dribbles a soccer ball in and out of the cones, with teams competing to get all their players through the fastest. If any team member hits a cone, he has to do ten jumping jacks — the consequence of unfair behavior.
- Round 2: Repeat the same drill, but if a team member hits a cone, the whole team has to do the jumping jacks — because the team is like your family, and your actions affect them.
- Round 3: Repeat the same drill again, but if a player hits a cone, all teams have to do jumping jacks, because your behavior affects your whole community.

Naz India
www.nazindia.org

Naz India engages teen girls at schools in low-income neighborhoods using team-based sports, including netball, a game similar to basketball. Naz India's Goal program provides life-skills training that covers health, safety, communication, financial literacy and leadership — including developing young women into peer-leaders and coaches. The following game builds body awareness and teamwork.

Body Ball
- A coach uses cones to mark a narrow, curving path about 6 m (20 ft.) long.
- Players pair up. They will work together to carry a ball from one end of the path to the other.
- To start, the coach calls out a body part that must be touching while the pairs carry the ball. For example, if the coach calls "hip-to-hip," players carry the ball down the path without breaking the contact between their hips.
- Repeat the exercise elbow-to-elbow, head-to-head, back-to-back and so on. Teams lose a point if they break contact or drop the ball, and win a point if they finish in the shortest time.

Top: Boys in the village of Mityana, Uganda, play with a banana-leaf ball.
Bottom: James (left) and Jack Arnold with a shipment of banana-leaf balls.

What You Can Do

Being a good sport on your own playground is a great way to make your community a better place. And fundraising for organizations like the ones in this book helps get coaches onto playgrounds in need around the world. That's what nine-year-old James and twelve-year-old Jack Arnold, brothers from Kansas City, Missouri, decided to do after meeting the parish priest of the village of Mityana, Uganda, who showed them photos of kids who made banana-leaf balls to play soccer. Realizing they had a love of sport in common, Jack and James decided to order some of these balls, sell them and send all proceeds back to the community. The money made from the banana-leaf balls helps fund school fees for village families who cannot afford them. For information, see www.bananaleaf.org.

PHOTO: FATHER VINCENT KAJOBA

PHOTO: JULIE ARNOLD